Oscar W. Humphrey

The Mystic World

Oscar W. Humphrey

The Mystic World

ISBN/EAN: 9783337376321

Printed in Europe, USA, Canada, Australia, Japan

Cover: Foto ©Andreas Hilbeck / pixelio.de

More available books at **www.hansebooks.com**

THE MYSTIC WORLD:

A LITERAL NARRATIVE OF STRANGE MYSTICAL OCCURRENCES, RARE MATER-
IALIZATIONS, VOICE SEANCES, CLAIRVOYANCE, CLAIRAUDIENCE,
TRANCE AND MENTAL PHENOMENA, SINGULAR PSYCHICAL
MANIFESTATIONS, THOUGHT TRANSFERRENCE, ETC.

The Locket Prophecy.

O. W. HUMPHREY,

A FOUNDER OF THE NATIONAL SPIRITUALIST ASSOCIATION,

WASHINGTON, D. C.,

1897.

CONTENTS:

O. W. Humphrey.

S INCERELY DEDICATED TO ALL WHO
LOVE AND DILIGENTLY SEEK FOR
TRUTH — IN WHATEVER FORM IT MAY
EXIST — FEARLESS OF CONSEQUENCES.·.

CHAPTER I.

Initiatory Experiences.

PILATE saith unto him: "What is truth?"

In the year 1882 my father made a journey to Washington, D. C., on certain business. He had relatives there who claimed to know that the spirits of departed mortals returned to communicate with the dwellers of the earth. When he returned he had with him a Spiritualist publication. He was a materialist. The shock of this discovery at an early period of life produced a strong impression on my mind. Battle after battle in the mental world has been fought. Every view, from every point possible, has been taken to prove the materialistic theory incorrect. Therefore, my interest was at once aroused by the publication which he brought with him.

In 1888 I made a visit to Washington. This was the beginning of my initiation into Spiritualism. In the old Grand Army Hall, corner Seventh and L streets northwest, Mr. Pierre Keeler invited a committee of skeptics upon the platform to examine slates on which writing would appear independently—that is, without other power than magnetism; the claim being that spirits would use the magnetic power of the medium to produce this writing. Three gentlemen stepped forward. Keeler sat at one end of the platform; the skeptics stood in the center. Presently a scratching sound was heard, and a peculiar shaking of the slates was observed. The three men had hold of the slates on which this took place. Keeler had merely touched them previously in plain sight to "magnetize" them, as he said. Two slates were held at a time, tied with a handkerchief. Several messages appeared on one slate in German and English, signed by different names. One of these gentlemen became a Spiritualist after this performance. Of the other two, one, I believe, expressed doubt; the other was bewildered. On the Wednesday following this, I took five new slates, which I had purchased on Seventh street, to Keeler's residence. There was a plain deal table in the room I entered. This table had no cover. Keeler sat at one side of the table; I sat opposite. I had previously prepared slips of paper containing questions addressed to deceased relatives and friends. I threw them on the table at Keeler's request. He touched them carelessly; then he said; "There is one (slip) here that does not belong to you." This was true. I had married while in Washington, and the slip Keeler referred to contained a question asked by my father-in-law inquiring about his uncle, Ezekiel, who had gone to Australia several years before and was reported to have died there. I do not remember the answer to this. Keeler said: "Here is another I can not get an answer to; throw it out." I did so. I threw it in the coal scuttle. He said: "Come to the hall next Sunday evening, and you will get an answer verbally to that." Before I left, I went to the coal scuttle, picked it up, and took it with me. Next Sunday evening he gave the name on this slip, although I had destroyed it, and what he told me as purporting to come from the spirit startled me by the nature of the message. The remaining slates contained short messages. One was signed by my step-mother's father, whom I had not addressed on a slip at all. He had died in 1871 in the northern section of New York. The writing on this slate, as it appeared, was: "I am happy to say a word. (Signed, Iram S———." The "m" in his first name is an error; it should be "Ira." Another slip which I had addressed to a former business associate of my father's was signed as I had written it—"Jack M———." I sent these slates to my father, who afterward stated that M——— never signed his name "Jack." It was always "John," and he showed me letters and documents in proof.

CHAPTER II.

A Vivid Impression.

MISS MARGARET GAULE is a well-known clairvoyant or "test" medium. She resides in Baltimore, Md., but travels about, and is particularly prominent in Washington. I met this lady at a friend's one evening. My wife and her mother were with me. Miss Gaule mentioned one or two names of spirits connected with my wife's mother and then turned to me. I had a short time before written an article addressed to a Spiritualist publication, but on reflection had destroyed it. She said: "I see two spirits standing near you. One is your mother, Laura—Laura Porter Humphrey. She is a slight person, with a dark complexion. You resemble her, and she died of consumption. She is a very beautiful spirit spiritually. The other was, when a mortal, an orthodox minister. He gives the name of George Tousley. He says his former views were erroneous; that he has received light since becoming a spirit, and seeks to remedy the wrong teachings of his mortal existence." Then the medium said: " 'Oscar, why did you destroy the article you wrote? It was inspirational. When we influence your mind, you must write. It is intended you shall do a great work for humanity.' These words are spoken by your mother.   Now they (the spirits) fade away and are gone.''   These words had a powerful effect on my mind.   I reflected: How was this woman able to speak my mother's full maiden and married name?   She had died thirty odd years before, at the age of twenty-one, in the State of New York, residing at the time in the Catskills.   Mr. George Tousley I did not know.   I had never heard of him.   Upon inquiry I learned that the medium's statement in regard to him was correct.   My wife's family had known him.   He had lived and died in the vicinity of my mother's home.   How did the clairvoyant know that I had destroyed an article written in the privacy of my room?   I had not given the matter a second thought.   From that time on I began to write for Spiritualist publications and to take an interest in Spiritualism. I believed that spirit return was a fact.   It was a great truth, a blessing to mankind, the greatest light of the age.   The character of my writings, prose and verse, was certainly of a peculiar nature, when it is reflected that I had previously never been accustomed to literary pursuits, and they really seemed to me to be born of inspiration.

CHAPTER III.

The Locket "Test."

ONE evening I attended a seance given by Miss Gaule at Wonn's Hall, on Sixth street northwest. I took with me a locket containing the fac-simile of my mother's face. This ornament I placed on the table standing on the platform before the medium arrived. After giving one or two "tests," she took up the locket, opened it, and said: "This locket belonged to a lady who died of consumption many years ago in the northern part of New York State." She then gave her name, and, looking toward me, said: "This spirit speaks to a young man in the audience—'Oscar, my son, do you not think your mother knows her own face when she sees it? Always keep this locket. *It will one day be the only proof you have that certain property is yours by right.*'" With this singular prophetic statement, and another which I will not refer to, the medium ceased to address me. The locket had been presented to me on my eighth birthday by my father.

I went to Miss Maggie subsequently for a private "sitting." I asked her what my mother meant by the words, "Always keep the locket. It will one day be the only proof you have that certain property is yours by right." She told me this property was so situated that it was impossible to secure it, and that nothing could be done till my father died, as he could only assist me after that event. She had previously predicted my father's death, saying his heart was affected, and that he would "pass away when the leaves fell again." Three years went by, however, before my beloved father left this sphere of action. He had complained of heart trouble, but finally succumbed to apoplexy.

CHAPTER IV.

The N. S. A.

THE National Spiritualist Association was organized primarily for the protection and furtherance of the interests of mediums and Spiritualists generally. I was interested in this movement, and wrote certain articles concerning it, and my name was placed on the committee having its formation in charge by the gentlemen whose names are inseparably connected with this important movement. Much has been said for and against the phenomenon of materialization or appearance of forms—the physical counterpart of departed mortals. The initial impetus of the N. S. A. was due to the antagonism of skeptics who made a savage attack on a professional medium for this phase, the medium being carried into a court of law on the charge of fraudulent practices by simulating ghosts of the dead. I shall not attempt an argument, but will relate my experience in this phase, leaving the readers of my narrative to form their own opinion. I wish to say, however, that I have not exaggerated the statements I make. What I write is a true and faithful account, and I will make affidavit of its truthfulness, and regard it as a matter of honor to state facts just as they occur.

• CHAPTER V.

The Emner Materializations.

ON one of the streets of the Nation's Capital, at the time I write, is a bicycle repair shop. If you should need a wheel repaired and were to inquire at the door as to terms, etc., you would be met by a nervous little man. You would be quick to notice that an eye had been injured, and if you were to know him intimately you would learn that the injury was caused by an electrical experiment, for he is an expert electrician.

This little man, if you were to approach him on the subject, could tell you of more strange experiences than the Psychical Society ever knew of in the way of ghosts, as old-time people called them, but which moderns term ''spirits,'' just as mesmerism has changed to hypnotism.

I know this little man and his wife well. Mr. and Mrs. J. R. Emner, Jr., are personal friends.

It so happened that in the spring of the year 1893 I received a friendly invitation from Mr. and Mrs. Emner to become a participant in a spirit-seance to be held in their home. Having heard rumors of strange doings, acceptance was not slow, and promptly at 8 o'clock a number of ladies and gentlemen had assembled to see and hear what might transpire.

About three years previously Mr. Emner's brother-in-law, Mr. Frank Creager, had departed from this kaleidoscopic realm for mansions in the skies. There had been a slight misunderstanding between Frank and Mr. Emner regarding the marriage of the former to the latter's sister, because Mr. Emner considered both too delicate in health and immature for betrothal. Frank's wife soon followed him, fully verifying Mr. Emner's foresight. Mr. Emner now felt very sorry for his action, although he had been right, and his peace of mind was much disturbed. As he was walking the street one day he met a friend who engaged him in conversation and related a peculiar experience he had had in a Spiritualistic way. Mr. Emner went home and told his wife, remarking that he thought the gentleman was a truthful man and of good judgment, and he would himself go to a Spiritualist gathering. So, on the following Sunday evening, he promptly presented himself for admission at the door of the old Grand Army Hall on Pennsylvania avenue. The medium of the occasion quickly informed him that Frank came to him as a spirit and stated that he bore no ill will toward him. On the contrary, he would be the means of bringing him good fortune. Mrs. Emner shortly after this went to a medium who received writings in closed envelopes. She received a communication from her deceased sister. Frank also ''materialized'' at this medium's home and promised to do so at Mrs. Emner's if she would comply with the proper conditions. She duly conformed with the requirements, and soon shadowy forms appeared, and other undeveloped phenomena took place, until finally solid semblances of human beings presented themselves for recognition. Frank made himself known by means of independent writings, Mrs. Emner's magnetic force serving as the the means of transmission, in which he gave instruction, warning, and advice. With this explanation I will describe what occurred, referring to notes taken at the time. Very few spirit mediums "materialize" forms unless screened from view. No photographer develops a photograph unless he goes into a dark room. The analogy is not perfect, but it serves to illustrate a law or principle not perfectly understood.

A piece of drapery was fastened across one corner of the little room where the seance took place, after those of the party who were so disposed had carefully examined the spot, behind which Mrs. Emner took her seat. She was in a delicate condition at the time, which must be taken into account when reading what follows. The room was small and led into a kitchen, open to inspection. The light was from an ordinary gas jet in this kitchen and cast its rays through the open door. It was slightly dimmed, but a newspaper could have been read without much trouble.

GHOST NO. 1.

After the preliminary exercises and a song, silence was observed; and just as the ladies began to get a trifle nervous the form of a young man, wearing a tightly-buttoned sack coat, his hands in the pockets of the garment, was seen to silently emerge from behind the drapery where sat Mrs. Emner. (Imagine the sensation to the nerves! It was a genuine ghost!) As he reached the doorway, where the light shone through, he paused; then passed out into the kitchen. I noticed that, as the forms reached this doorway, the light seemed to give them a shock, just as an electric battery would a mortal, and they seemed to make an effort to overcome this shock, the same as one would catch his breath facing a strong wind. The form, as I said, went into the outer room or kitchen, where he or it remained for perhaps sixty seconds, during which time my nerves, and, I presume, those of the rest of the invited party, were stretched to a high tension. Then the figure noiselessly returned and disappeared—vanished; that is the only way I can describe it—at or behind the curtain.

THE ACROBATIC GHOST.

A queer looking nondescript now presented itself, clothed in male attire. Its feet were bare, however. Passing across the room where we sat till he reached the opposite wall, he threw himself into the position of a boy about to turn a handspring. Up went a pair of slim bare ankles, the light shining full upon them, with a soundless, snaky movement. Anything more wierd and uncanny cannot be imagined. Then his feet touched the floor. Up and down they went, with a peculiar jerky hingelike motion at the hips, as if he were an automaton, not the slightest sound being audible when the feet touched wall or floor, until, apparently tired of his sport, he rolled on the carpet, and then arose and returned to the curtain. Let anyone without practice attempt to perform this feat of balancing and observe the discomfiture and racket that would ensue. Not even an expert could avoid a shuffling noise more or less noticeable. What, then, can be the opinion of those disposed to be critical, when the statement is repeated that Mrs. Emner was about to become a mother.

THE CADAVEROUS GHOST AND THE LITTLE GIRL.

Perhaps five minutes passed by—I do not know the exact time. Then came a ghost entirely different in appearance. He was an elderly man with a beard on his face and wearing a frock coat. His ankles seemed to be clad in white leggings, like a Frerch Zouave. I do not understand this. None of the figures spoke. X-rays are an apparent contradiction to the ordinary phenomenon of light. Another analogy. This spirit made a bee-line for the kitchen. In this kitchen we had stored our hats, overcoats, cloaks, etc. Returning, he had on his head a derby hat. In his hand he held a beaver. A rocking chair stood near the open door within, say, three feet of the sitters in his proximity. A little child, a girl, stood not far from the spirit. He quietly picked her up and seated himself in the rocker, taking the little tot on his knee. Then he began to rock, appearing to enjoy our amazement. The child's hair was caught up by a pink celluloid comb, hoop-shaped.   This the spirit took in his hand and reaching out to a gentleman placed it on his head, causing him to present a ludicrous appearance.   The beaver hat was also transferred to the nearest cranium, which it adorned with becoming grace. Thus he sat for perhaps ten minutes, possibly twenty.   We looked at him with all our eyes.   He had the appearance such as a man would have who had long suffered from illness or was just beginning to take on the sere and yellow leaf—that is, his arms and legs looked shrunken and his face cadaverous. Finally he arose and slowly ambled to the battery which generated the force sufficient for the time being to enable these inhabitants of another world to take on the material shell.

THE BURLY GHOST WHO ELBOWED AND SHOULDERED.

Like magic a burly powerfully-built figure now advanced, with a quick decided step.   Straight forward he came, without hesitation.   We sat around a table.   He bustled up to this table and commenced to elbow and shoulder the sitters without ceremony.   Everything was instantly confusion, and smothered laughs and nervous giggles, interspersed with whispered ejaculations, greeted the ghostly sally.   Nothing daunted, our jolly friend made the circuit of the table until he reached a young lady at the farther extreme.   Pausing, he clasped her beneath the shoulder blades and raised her from the floor. Her weight was certainly one hundred and fifty pounds, but she was lifted with the lightness and grace of an infant.

THE GHOST WHO PROMENADED THE TABLE.

On his heels came a tall slender young man. It is my impression that the preceding spirit had not yet left the vicinity of the table when its successor sprang lightly UPON IT. He held in his hand a long roll of paper. With this he good humoredly tapped first one and then another, turning quickly here and there. I arose from my seat, standing on my tip-toes, and, as I am somewhat tall and he stooped slightly, my eyes were on a level with his chin, so that I could observe his features. He had a long thin nose, an unusually sloping fore-head, and a moustache just beginning to sprout. Dancing about he at length scrambled off. By this time everyone was in hearty good humor and not a bit afraid.

THE LADY GHOST.

So far we had only gentlemen as visitors, but now came, with graceful demeanor, an appearance clad in the garb of the fair sex. With a charming sweep of the arms and an undu-lating poise of the body, she seemed as if waiting to be greeted. Some one passed her a fragrant American beauty rose. This she held to her nostrils with an air of delight. I observed particularly that her hair was *crimped* and floated about her shoulders. The ladies will appreciate my statement when I say that Mrs. Emner's hair was smooth and worn *closely coiled.* This final phenomenon of the evening wandered about the circle and then went the way of those preceding her.

Thus passed an evening the like of which may only be

found in a tale from the Arabian Nights. No language can describe the unearthly character of these visitants—human and yet not human.

All this time Mrs. Emner sat entranced. So far as she was concerned, she might as well have been at the North Pole or in the Tropics. I heard a faint voice emanating from the region of the curtain, which I was informed was Frank Creager's, Emner's brother-in-law, in the spirit world. One thing is certain—his grammar was perfect. It was that of an educated man. I distinctly noted that the construction of his sentences was not of the form used by Mrs. Emner. I had in my coat pocket a bill book containing papers. As an experiment, I passed this behind the curtain. Not a ray of light was there, yet instantly she stated the nature of its contents, reading correctly the first words of a newspaper article, which I kept in memory and afterward verified. In reality it was a little girl "controlling" Mrs. Emner who accomplished this remarkable feat. Mrs. Emner is a tall, somewhat large, woman, with generally poor health. She "sat" for a year without intermission and without regard to the thermometer before complete "development" was achieved. After her second child was born not a single spirit exhibited its ghostly presence in her domicile for perhaps two years, but at the time of writing (October, 1897,) these remarkable phenomena have again asserted themselves. I will say in conclusion that materialization is a delicate science and its development not easily accomplished, and requires, in addition, an inherent natural gift.

———

Having given an account of the seance I participated in and of the strange occurrences which took place, I will now repeat what Mr. and Mrs. Emner related to me. They have been frequent visitors at my home, and the "ghosts" have appeared there through Mrs. Emner's mediumship as well as in their own dwelling.

This couple were at one time dwellers in a certain domicile, No. —, —— street, which they had leased for some length of time. But they were not there long before curious events occurred. In one of the rooms of the house there was a dark brown stain about the length and breadth of a human being of average size. Strange to say, at various times this peculiar looking spot would become damp or moist. This was odd; but one night they were startled by a strong masculine voice saying:

"G—— d—— you! This is my grave, and you are standing on it! Get out of here."

They inquired who it was speaking, but received only curses in reply.

"Can we not pray for you?"

"To h—— with your prayers. I don't want any such d—— nonsense!"

"Well, what can we do for you?"

"Get out of here. We are going to drive you out!" the spirit exclaimed angrily. "You can't stay here."

Night after night shuffling footsteps were heard passing up and down stairs, and muttering voices were audible. Articles were violently thrown, and all sorts of annoyances took place. The neighbors were inquired of, and it was learned that once a man was killed in the house while gambling. The voice had finally consented to reveal its identity, and this was corroborated upon inquiry. The stain on the floor was blood. No one had ever been able to live in the house, although the rent had been reduced. Sickness, death, and misfortune came, and at last the electrician and his wife could stand it no longer and had to leave.

On the wedding night of my friends as strange a celebration as ever mortal man has experienced was theirs. As my friend's wife said:

"It is all foolishness to tell these things, for no one will believe them," but I will give the statements as related.

Just as the festivities were at their height, behold! a group of figures, short and tall, young and old, male and female, numbering perhaps fifty, suddenly formed and in grotesque procession flitted through the house, filed solemnly up stairs, lighted every gas jet, and then, one and all, they passed, vanished, in single file, through an upper window.

On one occasion there came the spirit of a gentleman who had been a suicide. He became addicted to drinking and gambling, abandoned his wife and child, and finally took his own life. In the meantime his wife and child had died. This spirit indicated that he was in distress—that is, in a psychic state involving punishment for his earthly misdeeds. He stated that he could occasionally see his wife and child at a distance, but could not reach them. As he expressed it, for every step he took forward he went back tenfold; but through the assistance of the good people in whose house he was he at last reached those he loved. My friend said the three appeared together one evening and whispered for an hour. The suicide said he could now occasionally be with his wife and child in spirit life, but was still forced to render equivalent for his former bad acts. He expressed his gratitude, and one night on opening the drawer of a bureau there lay a sum of money, forty-five dollars. Reverses of fortune had rendered money a desirable article, but the sight of those substantial U. S. greenbacks created fright. The suicide calmed their fears—"that money," said he, "I buried just before I died. It is true I won it at gambling, but take it. It is all right. It is yours for what you have done for me. I dug it up and brought it here." That was the last time the spirit appeared. He never would reveal his identity. At another time, however, a sum something like twenty-five dollars was found in the house when greatly needed; but the most curious happening was that when one evening they desired to go to an entertainment. On a piece of paper they read the words: "You are going to the entertainment to-night." They laughed and said, "How can we go without money?" "You will certainly go," was written; "look on the table." Judge of their surprise to see a one-dollar bill suddenly appear. The tickets to the entertainment cost fifty cents each. Shortly afterward they were told that this dollar bill was given them by a spirit who had taken on the material form in the city of Pittsburg, not in a cabinet, nor even in a house, but out on the open street. This spirit said he was walking along the street when he was accosted by a man out of work. The spirit told this man he had no work for him (naturally), but he could tell him where to get a job. The man felt so grateful that he asked the supposed mortal to meet him again and he would give him all he could spare of the first money he earned. But the spirit took only the dollar, and this dollar he gave to his host of the evening.

When manifestations first began to occur in their presence, the gentleman one evening asked that some strong proof be given them. ''Go outside,'' was written, ''and close by the door you will find a five-cent piece.'' The money was found, verifying the statement made. A hole was drilled in it and a ribbon passed through. This keepsake was worn by the gentleman's sister until her decease, and was buried with her. A promise has been given that this same five-cent piece will be returned to them. It has been raised, they have been told, about half way up through the ground.

I will conclude the account of these astounding phenomena with one further incident.

At one of the seances to which I was invited, but did not attend, Mr. Emner states that an elderly lady materialized wearing old-fashioned goggle-glasses. These were passed about among the sitters, handled freely, and returned. That was the last seen of them. I have in my possession, however, a shred of hair that a spirit plucked from his beard, while standing at my elbow. I examined this under a microscope in comparison with my little boy's. It was coarser and darker, but otherwise not distinguishable.

CHAPTER VI.

The Colored Medium.

A YOUNG colored man, an oyster shucker of Washington, named Basel Lockwood, caused much comment at one time by his peculiar mediumistic powers. A number of friends were invited to my home one evening to witness an exhibition of his gifts. He was first securely tied by means of ropes fastened to rings screwed into the walls and floor, and the light turned down. We all joined hands and, after a short intermission filled up by singing, during which beautiful lights appeared, one of the ropes was laid gently in my lap, although I sat across the room opposite the medium. Presently the remaining ropes were also untied, the light was turned up, and the medium found entirely free. A pair of new handcuffs were now produced by a gentleman well known in Washington. He stated no duplicate key could be used, as each pair of irons had a differently-constructed mechanism. (These handcuffs came from the city court house, being used to confine prisoners, and were loaned for the occasion.) The colored man's neck was now tied to a ring in the wall, the irons locked on his wrists, the key placed on a stand in the center of the room under a bell, and the light again turned down. Almost directly the bell began to ring, keeping time with the singing, the key was heard to click in the locks, and the hand-cuffs fell on the floor; whereupon the light was turned up, the medium found with his neck still fastened to the wall and his hands free.   Mr. Lockwood's hands were next tied behind his back as securely as possible, the light turned down, and almost instantly he called out to have the light turned on. There he appeared with his coat partially removed, one sleeve being entirely off his arm, but his hands were still tied as they had been.   The light was again lowered and immediately raised, whereupon the coat was found in its proper place, buttoned from top to bottom.   On a subsequent evening, at the house of a friend, Basel was seated in a chair about six feet from the wall.   A long rope was then wound around him till he could move neither hand nor foot.   One end of the rope was then carried back to a ring screwed firmly in the wall and fastened thereto.   The other end was carried out in front about twelve feet to where the visitors sat.   A piece of stout thread was then knotted about his wrists.   My wife and I held the end of the rope extending out to us, so that the slightest movement would have betrayed him.   The light was lowered, yet in less than five minutes he called for it to be turned up, and we saw him with one sleeve of his coat re-moved and turned inside out, but the rope was precisely as we had left it, being still wound about the colored phenomenon, and his wrists were still confined by the packthread.   This young man of peculiar qualities was afterward the hero of the Ford Theatre disaster, saving a number of lives by his bravery and skill.

CHAPTER VII.

𝔐iscellany.

AN ODD EXPERIENCE.

IN the year 1865-6 my parents resided in the city of Daven-
port, Iowa. I was at that time a child between five and six
years of age. One morning, just as day was dawning, having
awakened, I lay quietly waiting for my parents to arouse.
Of a sudden, the figure of a man stepped from behind the
stove at the other side of the room. The pipe of the stove
ran up nearly as high as the ceiling. A paroxysm of fright
instantly seized me. Perspiration burst from every pore of
my skin, the hair of my head seemed to rise from its scalp,
and my tongue clove to the roof of my mouth. With the
greatest effort I reached my right hand to my father's shoulder, who lay next to me, and gasped:

"Father, father!"

It seemed an age till my parent awoke, for I was in mortal
terror lest the apparition should come all the way across the
room, it having already crossed half way. Having become
awake, my father inquired what the matter was.

"There is a man standing there," I replied.

He gave a hasty, drowsy glance, and remarked that he saw no one.

"Oh, yes, there he is. Don't you see him? There he stands!"

Finding that I would not be pacified, my father arose and started toward the stove. As he did so, the figure quickly receded, to my great relief, and stood behind the stove. Here the personage stood, and in grim humor, evidently delighting in my dismay, commenced to oscillate sidewise, peering first from one side and then the other of the stove-pipe, just as a mischievous person will to plague a child. Its movements were volatile and noiseless. It seemed to glide, and yet float. As my father reached the center of the room, the image, with a quick, darting movement, dashed toward a closed door opening on a hallway, giving a parting look as he went, and seemed to go through the door.

All this occurred within the space of a minute or so, and when my frightened ejaculations had informed my father of the disappearance of the cause of the disturbance, he chided me for what he thought was an unnecessary alarm, and returned to his bed. My childish mind could not understand the occurrence, and it might have always remained a mystery were it not that I became acquainted with the manifestations incident to Spiritualism.

MENTAL PHENOMENA.

For those who delight in the strange and curious, I will tell of an incident that occurred in my experience with

One night I awoke and lay quietly thinking, as is my custom, when suddenly there flashed across my mind the words "Robert Gilmore," and closely following, "Fredericksburg, Ohio." So vivid was the impression that I kept the words in memory and next day looked for "Fredericksburg, Ohio," in the postal guide. I found the place and then wrote to the postmaster there, asking if "Robert Gilmore" lived in that city. I received the following reply:

"Fredericksburg, O., Feb. 2, '96.

"There is no Robert Gilmore here, but there is a John and George Gilmore; but they are not in any business.

"Yours respectfully,

"JOHN H. OWINGS."

———

I then wrote to John Gilmore, asking him if he knew Robert Gilmore, and whether he was deceased or living. He replied as follows:

"Fredericksburg, O., Feb. 12, '96.

"Dear Sir: I have an uncle by the name of Robert Gilmore, but I have never seen him, nor don't know whether he is living or dead. Don't know where he is.

"J. O. GILMORE."

———

In November of '96 I published the incident concerning "Robert Gilmore" in a journal devoted to Spiritualism, and next month there appeared in the same publication this statement:

MENTAL PHENOMENA.

In the last issue of your paper I saw an inquiry about Robert Gilmore, but do not know that he is the person I knew years ago. Robert Gilmore was the son of Harvey Gilmore, of Newark, O., (my old home). I think his mother's name was Lucy. He went to Zanesville, and owned and edited a paper there (I forget the name). He married Maria Cox. She died and he married again. I knew his first wife well, but not the second. I heard that Robert died many years ago, but know not where. If Robert is still living, he must be very old, for I am 73, and we were children together, he being some years the oldest. Robert's father moved to Iowa, I think to Glenwood, with his second wife (Miss Nancy Bridges, my old teacher). It is many years since I met or have thought of this family, as I left Newark in 1857.

MRS. C. V. BLACKMAN.

Pittsburg, Kan.

———

January 30, 1897, I published a statement, saying:

"It is now definitely ascertained that Mr. Robert Gilmore is a spirit. Mrs. S. S. Curtis, of New York City, has written me that she was acquainted with the gentleman for a number of years, and was at his bedside when he passed out of the body. She wishes to communicate with Mrs. C. V. Blackman, of Pittsburg, Kan., who also wrote that she knew Mr. Gilmore, and this may assist the spirit to reach his friends in mortal life. I have requested that she publish the result of their joint effort, as I wish to present an argument in favor of spirit control versus purely mental phenomena.''

I regret to state that I have never heard further concerning Mr. Robert Gilmore. The incident presents an unsolved problem which time and circumstance may explain.

WAS IT THOUGHT TRANSFERRENCE?

The following incident came under my observation:

On Friday evening, June 2, '93, a young married woman, visiting her aunt at E—— was taken suddenly ill. Violent convulsions, with vomiting, seized her. This was at 8 o'clock p. m. She seemed to be at the point of dissolution, and a physician was hastily summoned. She did not die, but two hours later, it being still feared she would not survive, it was decided to telegraph her parents in the northern part of ——. The telegram was addressed to her father and was worded: ''E—— is very ill. Come at once.'' When the message was taken to the telegraph office, however, the manager stated that a telegram would not arrive at its destination before 7 o'clock the next morning, as the office at the receiving point was closed for the night. The convulsions, under the influence of an anæsthetic previously given, finally wore away, and the sufferer began to recover; so the telegram was not sent.

On the following Friday, June 9th, the young lady received a letter from her mother. In this letter the mother related a dream she had the previous Friday night (June 2d), the date

of her daughter's illness.   She dreamed that a telegram had
been received addressed to her husband, saying their daughter
was dead, and requesting him to come and get the body.   The
mother further dreamed that her husband then started on his
journey to bring the corpse home for burial, and that she saw
the coffin arrive.

This was the dream, substantially as told in the letter, and
the mother advised her daughter to be careful, as she knew
her dreams came true.   No communication had been trans-
mitted between the two dates, June 2d and 9th, as it was not
thought advisable to cause unnecessary alarm after the recov-
ery, except a letter sent by the daughter, which was mailed
June 8th; but this was not received by the mother till 3
o'clock, p. m., June 9th, whereas the mother's letter was
mailed at 10 a. m., June 9th.   So the mother had no information previous to mailing her letter.

The question suggests itself: What caused the mother's
singular corroboratory dream?

Neither mother nor daughter profess Spiritualism.

HE WAS CONSCIOUS.

A singular clairvoyant test was once given by a well-known
medium concerning a member of my wife's family.   Her
grandfather had been stricken with paralysis, and apparently
passed through the final throes of dissolution.   He was of the
orthodox faith, and was utterly skeptical concerning spirit-
return.   However, he was persuaded, previous to his final

leave-taking, to return as a spirit and give a test of his pres-
·ence. On Monday he was buried in the soil of Virginia. On
the following Friday evening my wife's parents attended a
public seance in Washington. At that time my wife's father
was a stranger to the medium. No sooner, however, did the
seance begin than the medium addressed herself to him. It is
necessary to state that my wife's grandfather had a brother,
Ezekiel, who a number of years before went to Australia and
died there. The medium said: ''I see an old gentleman coming up the aisle, leaning on the arm of his brother, Ezekiel,
who died years ago in Australia. They come to you, sir,''
pointing to my wife's father, ''and the elderly gentleman who
leans on the arm of Ezekiel is your father. He says, 'New-
ton, I have come as I agreed. (Then followed a beautiful
description of his reception in spirit life.) You all thought I
was out of my mind when I was talking with my two sisters,
Ruth and Lucinda (they had died seventy years before); but
it was so. And I want to say this: I did not die at eleven
o'clock, as you supposed. (He had had the third and last
shock.) I was conscious and tried to make you know I was
still alive. The cloth was tied so tight around my face (to
keep the jaw from falling) that I suffered torture until six
o'clock next morning (seven hours) when my spirit left my
body. I did not believe in your way of thinking, but now I
find you were right. Go on with your good work, and God
bless you!' '' The final words of his test, ''God bless you,''
were a common expression. Then the medium said: ''Why,

that spirit is not buried yet! Yes, it is just buried, for I see a newly-made grave in Virginia.'' Of course, while my wife's family were gratified to receive such evidence of the old gentleman's presence, they were deeply grieved over its peculiar character. Next evening a lady well known in Spiritualistic circles as a medium was invited to their home. This lady was unacquainted with the facts just related. My wife's grandfather manifested his presence and strove to calm the unhappy state of mind caused by his statement in regard to his having been conscious when he was laid out for burial. He said his principal horror was lest he should be buried while still conscious; but, happily, this did not occur. He expressed himself as happy in his new abode, and his soothing words had their due effect.

Thus the facts are presented of two clairvoyants, one corroborating the statements of the other, yet neither was personally acquainted with the circumstances as they occurred, nor were they associated with each other. Altogether it was a remarkable attestation of spirit existence.

A BUSINESS MAN'S TALE.

A gentleman of my acquaintance, whom I shall designate as Mr. X., related to me the following singular account:

Some seven years previous to the time of writing, Mr. X. started in business for himself in one of the principal cities. He had saved a small sum of money while working as a mechanic, which he utilized to start with, and immediately incurred an indebtedness of several hundred dollars, and was able to maintain his standing only by a hard struggle; but he persevered and gradually overcame his difficulties.

In a short time he had canceled his debt, bought stock in the concern whose work he was doing the principal share of, purchased a piece of ground in a good business location, and erected a suitable building in which to carry on his enterprise.

This gentleman is an enthusiastic psychist, and his acts are governed by his own psychical powers and his knowledge of Spiritualistic phenomena.

Apparently there was nothing extraordinary in what he had so far accomplished. It would seem that anyone with good fortune, industry, and business sagacity could have been equally successful, but subsequent events leave the question open for debate whether there are not forces outside the material that enter into and govern the affairs of men, and by so doing explain why one man wins and another fails.

The subject of this narrative, Mr. X., soon found that his success was envied and that efforts were being made to accomplish his ruin. One man tried to force him into a position where he would be obliged to relinquish what stock he had purchased in the concern which had been the main element of his success. Had the intention been accomplished, Mr. X.'s downfall would have been immediate. He was warned of this through a medium, and by quick action was able to thwart the malevolent purpose. But this was not the only instance of sinister designs frustrated, and in their results lie the peculiarity of this narrative.

Mediums informed Mr. X. that he had an unusually strong force of spirit advisers interested in his welfare, and they would assist and protect him. His various enemies were worsted in every conceivable manner. One man was paralyzed, another died, another lost all his property. In fact, no less than nine different men who had endeavored to ruin him were themselves the victims of misfortune. One of these men, who sought to entangle him in meshes from which he could not escape, became ill. A certain spirit informed Mr. X. through a medium that those who guarded his welfare were going to cause this man's death. "But," said Mr. X., "I don't want this man harmed."

"You have nothing to do with it," was the prompt response. "Attend to your own affairs and we will attend to ours."

Mr. X., however, so far disregarded his spirit friend's somewhat arbitrary injunction as to go to the man who had sought to injure him and endeavored to remove the baneful influence. Mr. X. admonished this evil-disposed personage that if he would not antagonize him further his illness would disappear. The wrong-doer promised to cease his antagonism, and from that hour began to improve and was soon well. How he was convinced that Mr. X. had the power to control his condition cannot be stated. In some way the light dawned on his mind that he was the victim of his own wrong-doing, but he doubtless did not know that his discomfiture emanated from an occult source.

Mr. X. to-day has a surplus of several thousand dollars, owns a fine residence, and keeps a large force of employees busy.

FATHER W——, A CATHOLIC PRIEST.

A certain Mrs. W——, herself a Protestant at one time but latterly a disciple of Spiritualism, had a brother-in-law, Father W——, a clergyman of the Roman Church, who died in California a few years previous to the time of writing.

At one of the trumpet seances given by Mr. and Mrs. Hibbits, of Muncie, Ind., Father W—— manifested.

"I am Father W——," he said, speaking through the trumpet. "I want you," addressing a gentleman and his wife, "to convey a message for me to Mrs. W——, my sister-in-law." He then stated what he desired to have conveyed.

Some one asked if he were not a Catholic.

"Yes," he said. "I was a Catholic on earth, and I am a Catholic still. The religion of Spiritualism is nearer that of Catholicism than anything else."

The gentleman and his wife to whom this spirit made himself known were acquainted with Mrs. W——, but they were unfamiliar with Father W——, except that they had a slight recollection of having heard his name mentioned, and they were at the time total strangers to Mr. and Mrs. Hibbits, it being their first visit at their seances.

CHAPTER VIII.

A Trumpet or Voice Seance.

AT 2 o'clock of a dismal, rainy, cold afternoon in November, 1896, my wife and I found ourselves in the seance-room of a Western trumpet medium visiting Washington, Mrs. E. S. Hibbits. As we entered a glance showed us a few people sitting in chairs ranged in a circle in the center of the room, which was otherwise bare of furniture except a wardrobe and a lounge. Heavy blankets covered the three windows, to exclude all light when the seance should begin, and two horns or trumpets, composed of tin, about four feet long and perhaps four inches wide at the flaring end, while the mouthpiece was quite small, stood within the circle. At the hour for the seance to take place, the people present—twelve ladies and eight gentlemen—were requested to arise and recite the Lord's Prayer. Then some one was asked to start a hymn. The medium and her husband sat with the rest. Both are old-fashioned people. They joined hands with the others. Their voices were frequently heard while spirits were conversing. Scarcely had the song ceased when a lisping childish voice spoke. It was a sweet little voice, and she called "papa," and her name was "Maggie." A kiss from the trumpet greeted our ears, and her papa inquired:

"Maggie, were you in my bed-room last night?"

"Yes, papa."

"What happened?"

"Why, papa, Johnnie was frightened, and you got up and went to his bed and lay down with him."

"Yes; well, what else happened?"

"Why, I threw a paper, and you jumped and thought it was the cat."

"That is right. Now sing the little song you used to sing," and the small quavering voice sang a quaint simple melody, and then, with a "good bye, papa; if I don't see you again, merry Christmas," she kissed and departed.

My own name was presently called. "Oscar," spoke a faint voice. Every person in the room was an absolute stranger to me except one lady, and she invariably addressed me by my surname; and I had previously cautioned my wife not to address me by name. The voice was weak, but I caught the name of a relative, and she had a request to make which was of itself a test. However, nearly all the voices were strong and plainly heard. When they first speak through a trumpet, they are usually weak, but after one or two trials gain strength. Male and female voices came and went in rapid succession. I was informed that the spirits manifesting raised the trumpets from the floor in some manner while speaking through them. Much of the language spoken was

German, and the conversation was mostly in regard to matters of interest to the sitters. Valuable information would be given or a consoling message concerning some matter of apprehension or trouble, usually of a material nature. These voices talked as easily and naturally as though their owners still inhabitated the physical body, the only unnatural feature being the laugh. One could easily distinguish the voices as speaking from the trumpet, from the peculiar sound. Sometimes a spirit requested a sitter to sing. Again, some spirit would offer a pretty verse in rythmic cadence that used to be a favorite in mortal life, and two of the spirits, apparently of highly developed attributes, sang with exquisitely rich tone, which conveyed an impression to me of something beyond mortal experience—of a world of refined beauty and harmony. One German spirit requested ''Ein deutches lied.'' When it was sung, he quickly said: ''Dast ist nicht recht. Du hast einen vers ausgelassen.'' And, sure enough, one verse had been omitted, from lapse of memory, and was quickly supplied by the spirit. Then ''Red Leaf,'' an American Indian, I was informed, who had a mighty voice, the strongest of all, shouted a war-whoop as only Indians can and chanted in Indian fashion; and Katie Kinsey, a sweet-voiced spirit, rendered a beautiful poem and invocation, and this closed the seance. These two, with a spirit named Dr. Sharpe, who had a dry, matter-of-fact, sonorous voice, were the controlling spirits.

From what I subsequently learned, there is a method or

science in spirit phenomena, and spirits who are adepts, and who gain their skill by long experience and close application, just as mortals do, study this art or science.

We sat in intense darkness, but the spirits could see plainly. Red Leaf stated without hesitation the relative positions of the sitters, calling their names without a mistake; and many other evidences were given that they could see.

One of the ladies present, a former native of the West Indies, who was the only person in the circle known to me, was visited by the spirit of an old lady, Maria Petersen, who had in mortal life been a resident of the Island of St. Thomas, a Danish possession. As a test, she requested the spirit to sing a Danish love song which they both were acquainted with. It was promptly rendered and recognized.

These seances created profound astonishment and much comment in Washington. Mr. Hibbits informed me subsequently that they had traveled thousands of miles, giving hundreds of seances, at which as many as twenty different languages had been spoken.

CHAPTER IX.

My Father's Death.

I WILL now revert to the verbal message of Miss Margaret Gaule in Chapter III, purporting to emanate from my spirit mother.

"Always keep this locket. It will one day be the only proof you have that certain property is yours by right," and also to her statement in regard to my father.

July 22, 1896, my father's death took place. On the evening previous I had a very uneasy feeling, and, although the rain began to pour down, I mounted my bicycle in order to attend a seance given by Mr. J. H. Altemus, residing in Washington and well known for his mediumistic talents. He gave me a singular "test," but said nothing concerning my father, although at that very hour, as I learned next day, he had been taken ill. Mr. Altemus said: "I see a very strange sight. I see a number of lovely ladies forming themselves in a circle. Now I see a band of Indians. They too form a circle. They all pass around you, marching and counter-marching and intermingling in a beautiful manner. I do not know what it means." Next day I received a telegram, but when I arrived my father was a corpse. Now that my father

had succumbed to the Great Destroyer I felt a strong incli-
nation to fathom the mystery of the old-fashioned tiny gold
locket. I again attended a seance held by Mr. Altemus. He
described my father accurately and the manner of his death,
but stated his condition as a new-born spirit was that of feeble-
ness and that he was unable to make the effort to say all he
would like. I next attended the trumpet seance described in
Chapter VIII. My father, as I have stated, died in July. The
trumpet or voice seance was given the following November.
My father did not manifest at this trumpet seance (November), but he did manifest at another held in March following,
1897. I shall describe this latter manifestation in proper
order.

CHAPTER X.

His Second Manifestation.

THE next seance I attended was a public one given by Miss Margaret Gaule. It is necessary to state that my father's body had been taken to the northern part of New York State for burial. On this occasion I took with me my father's Masonic ring and the locket enclosed in an envelope. I placed this envelope on a small table standing on the platform previous to the medium's arrival. When the seance began she turned to me and commenced to relate that she saw the spirit of a large man, who placed his hand to his head as if in pain, and who, she said, died of apoplexy; and that a miniature banner appeared to her clairvoyantly, which presently was torn to shreds. "Ah, now I see what it means!" she exclaimed. "Long ago you sent your father a publication called the 'Banner.'" "I" (speaking for the spirit) "read what it said of Spiritualism, but would not gratify you, my son, with that knowledge, and tore the paper into shreds." (This action was characteristic of my father, who had a hasty temper, although of a jovial disposition.) Then the spirit went on to say that he regretted not knowing what he did in his present state, and expressed his gratitude for the efforts I had made in his behalf.   After the medium had given one or two tests more, she picked up the envelope containing the ring and locket, and said: "There are two articles in this inclosure, each belonging to a separate individual, which makes it diffi- cult for me to give a reading, as their magnetisms are mixed, but I will try.   I see before me a large gentleman, a newly arisen spirit, for I see a fresh-made grave.   Now I see a very beautiful spirit—that of a lady.   In this envelope is a locket containing a picture of this lady.   Now I see her draw from the finger of the gentleman that stands by her side a ring, and this ring is that which is also in the envelope."   The medium then held the package up and asked whose it was.   I arose and stated it was mine, and that her two tests, or both parts of one test, were correct; whereupon she asked me to place the articles in her hand minus the envelope.   She then spoke of my father having been buried by Masons far north; that I was not present, though I made the effort to be with him when he passed away, and she described a sheaf of wheat—a Masonic emblem—which had been thrown in upon the casket. This was literally true.   I did not know it was a Masonic emblem until the medium made the statement.   My brother- in-law is a Mason, and he had the token carried to the grave, where it rested after the casket had been lowered, having been overlooked.   I directed his attention to it, and it was then thrown down upon the casket.

As I have stated, this was a public seance.   Subsequently I attended another, accompanied by my step-mother, whom I wished to interest in Spiritualism. The spirit of my father came as before. The medium repeated almost literally the test I have related, only instead of the sheaf or bunch of wheat she spoke of the fragrant flowers placed on the casket, and how delicious their perfume had been to the spirit. This time I had the ring in my vest pocket, but did not carry with me the locket. Miss Gaule clairvoyantly saw this ring, and requested me to hand it to her. Upon receiving it she smiled and stated my father wanted to know why I did not wear it on my finger instead of in my pocket, and that he advised me to take the Masonic degrees. This concluded the test.

CHAPTER XI.

My Father's Voice.

I WILL now relate the occurrences at the trumpet seance of March, 1897. At this seance my father spoke apparently with his own voice, and this description is by far the most interesting of all my experiences, and of vital importance in the sequence of the locket spirit messages.

The second time the Hibbits visited Washington (March, 1897), they held their seances on 11th street northwest, between F and G. I made an engagement to be there at 2 o'clock. They held their regular seance at this hour each day. I arrived early, and as it was tedious to pass the time I went out, strolled into a barber shop and had my hair cut. When I returned, it was past the hour for the seance to begin and I was forced to take a seat in the seance-room close to the door outside the "circle." The manager of the circle had manifested some displeasure at my coming late, and I thought I would get no message. Presently, however, a childish spirit voice that had been addressing some one in the circle called out:

"Man, I say man! I want the man by the door."

Now, it was pitch dark, and I could not see a solitary object. The voice said:

"Come up close to the circle. I want you to sit by my papa."

I hitched my chair in the direction of where I supposed the 'circle'' to be, and finally reached some one, I did not know who.

"You are not sitting by my papa. Move farther along,'' spoke the voice.

I made another move, and a gentleman reached out his hand in my direction and touched me. I thought I recognized the voice as that of "Maggie'' in the former trumpet seance, described in Chapter VIII, and such it was. So I said:

"Is that you, Maggie? How did you like what I wrote about you?'' (I had published an account of the seance at the time.)

She made some casual reply, and said:

"You did not think when you sat by the door any one would come to-day and speak to you. I know why you felt bad. I saw you when you went out.''

I asked Maggie why I felt bad. She said because Mr. Hibbits scolded, and admonished him to be more mild in his address. I did not dispute the little spirit, but asked her where I went. She stated correctly and that she was with me. I inquired what the barber said to me.

"He asked you if you wanted a ''poo.' ''

"A 'poo?''

"Yes; a shampoo."

"And what did I say to him?"

"You said no, for you thought you would be late, and you was late. Your papa is coming to-day."

"All right, Maggie; you bring him," and the little voice ceased.

Directly a masculine voice startled me by calling out: "Oscar!" in a deep undertone.

"Who is it?" I asked.

"Luman."

"Luman who?"

"Luman Humphrey."

"What relation were you to my father?"

"His brother."

"What was my mother's name?"

"Laura Porter Humphrey."

"What was her middle name?"

"Laura Anna Porter."

Now, I never knew my mother's full middle name. My grandmother had once sent me a braid of her hair in oval form attached to a card, and on this card was inscribed "Laura A. Porter." The "A" coincides with "Anna."

"Well, Uncle Luman, is my father coming to-day?"

"Yes. You have had something on your mind for a long time. You came here to-day to get some information from him about this matter—a business matter. He is going to tell you all about it. I am going now, so that he can talk to you."

[This uncle manifesting was a surprise to me. He died when a very young man. It was his first manifestation.]

The room was silent for a moment, and then a weak vibrating voice sent a thrill to my heart by uttering my name in a hoarse gutteral whisper.

"Father, is that you? I am very glad to hear you speak;" and then, after a few common-place exchanges of greeting, I asked:

"Father, what have I in my pocket?"

"A locket."

"What does that locket contain?"

"Your mother's picture. It is an old-fashioned locket. They are not worn nowadays."

"Well, father, what else is in the locket?"

[It so happened the locket had contained both of my parents' likenesses, but I had removed that of my father, and in its place rested the braid of hair before mentioned for safe keeping.]

Said the voice, speaking through the trumpet, "Why did you remove my picture?"

"Well, father, what did I put in its place?" I asked, laughing.

He correctly replied: "Your mother's hair."

"Well, father, are you going to tell me anything about the property connected with the locket to-day?"

"I am not strong enough to-day, but I will the next time you come."

"Shall I come privately?"

"No; come the same as you do now" (meaning a public seance).

"Shall I come next Sunday?"

"Yes; I guess that will do. Good bye, I am going now," and the voice ceased.

The following Sunday I again attended the trumpet seance, but, strange to say, not a word was spoken to me. I believe I was the only exception, and there was no explanation. I waited until Wednesday and again took my place in the "circle," and this time a faint voice whispered my name.

"Is it you, father?"

"Yes, my son."

"How is mother Laura? Is she coming to-day?"

"Your *mamma* is going to speak to you."

"Well, what have you to say about the locket matter? You said you were going to tell me all about it."

"You will —— —— —— on paper," and with a faint ringing sound the trumpet dropped to the floor.

Now, this voice was not my father's at all. It was a woman's voice. Furthermore, my father never in his life used the term "mamma." He taught me when a child to say "mother." I did not catch clearly the sentence, "You will —— —— —— on paper." To my mind this manifestation was for some unexplained reason a well-intentioned simulation by a female spirit. The voice was sweet and low.

At the previous seance my father's voice and words were thoroughly characteristic of him. I had said to him then:

"You did not believe this once."

"No, I would not listen to you. Now, I want you to listen to me. The property you want to know about does not amount to much, and it will take a great deal of hard work to get it."

He had spoken about my health on that occasion. I had a severe cold at the time. He said to me:

"You are not well. Place flannel on your chest and wear rubbers in damp weather."

I had always been subject to weak bronchial tubes, and during his mortal life my father insisted, in adverse weather, on my wearing a chest protector, and, if damp, a pair of rubbers.

The spirit voice speaking through the trumpet apparently was aware that I detected the imposition, for, as I have stated, the trumpet dropped to the floor with a muffled ring, and that was all I heard the remainder of the seance.

That was the last of the trumpet seances I attended, as the Hibbits shortly afterward went to their home in Muncie. I inferred that I would, perhaps, get the information I wished for on paper in some manner, according to the words, "You will —— —— —— on paper."

CHAPTER XII.

The Mysterious Paper.

SHORTLY after the events related in the last chapter, my wife visited Mr. Altemus, the medium, at his home. Among other things, he told her there was a certain "paper" in a desk. This desk, he said, was in the house at N——, the residence of my father's family. It stood near a window, and the paper was in a drawer on the right-hand side. He said the paper was of value to me and advised us to obtain it. His description of this desk was excellent. We knew the desk well. This clairvoyant message was obtained in May, 1897. In June following I visited a gentleman, a medium of Washington. He said, after some preliminary descriptions of spirits which were indefinite and not recognized clearly:

"You came in search of hidden property. The spirit of a lady comes here. She perished of a consumptive and asthmatic ailment. She shows me a locket with her picture in one side, and the other side has something removed."

I acknowledged the description as that of my mother, and I told him of the statement once made by a medium concerning the locket and asked him if he could tell me anything about it.

"Yes," he said; "this property came direct from your

mother. It is situated near New York City on an island. Your father jeopardized the title by allowing a paper to slip from his hands. Your mother wants me to trace this matter.''

I remarked that my father had stated it did not amount to much and would take a good deal of hard work to get it. (This was at the trumpet seance.)

"On the contrary," said the medium, "it has increased until it is very valuable."

CHAPTER XIII.

"Tim."

THE following month, July, 1897, I went to Mr. Altemus myself. The gentleman has a control known as "Tim." Tim is an Irishman and speaks a thorough brogue. A "control" in Spiritualism means a spirit who controls or has possession of a medium and speaks through the medium, the medium being in an unconscious or "trance" condition. Mr. Altemus is a personal acquaintance and Tim knew me well. He talked about things occurring in my home—my most private affairs—in a way that showed he had been there frequently (admitting the verity of spirit existence). I cannot reproduce Tim's blarney perfectly, it being inimitable. Said he:

"Ye kem to inquire about the property."

"Yes, Tim. Has the locket anything to do with it?"

"Yer mother's picter is in the locket, and b' the powers, it was from her ye got it."

At that moment the medium, who was opposite the table at which we had seated ourselves, burst into tears. (It was Tim who wept.)

"O, Oscar, Oscar, do not be angry with me. It was a mistake to let the paper slip away."

The next moment Tim had recovered himself, and he said:

"It was yer father threw that condition upon me. Let by-gones be by-gones, friend. Yer father says ye shall recover the property. 'Harvey' is here. He will help you get the property to expiate the acts he committed in mortal life.''

Now, I have a deceased relative by marriage whose first name is "Harvey," with whom I was a favorite when a boy, but who was not noted for treading the straight and narrow path, he being of a jovial nature akin to Burns' Tam O'Shanter.

"Well, Tim, how about the paper in the desk that your medium told about?''

"The paper has been removed. The leddy (meaning my wife) should have gone before.''

"Where is the paper now, Tim?''

"In another desk.''

"At the office?''

"Yes, in the room where the flat-top stove is, close by the bookcase.''

I recognized the little barrel-like flat-top stove. The bookcase, I afterward learned, was situated as Tim had stated.

"Can I find the paper now, Tim?''

"Begorrah, I'll help ye find the paper! I'll go with ye! I'll help ye find it,'' Tim ejaculated, excitedly.

"All right, Tim.''

"I say, friend, why don't ye search the records where yer mother died?''

I told Tim I did not know the precise locality where my mother had passed away, but would inquire; and after some further conversation, not important, the seance closed.

CHAPTER XIV.

𝕿𝖍𝖊 𝕾𝖊𝖆𝖗𝖈𝖍.

A FEW days after my conversation with Tim I went to N——. I went to the office. The desk was *gone*. I asked where it was. It had been sold. What became of the contents? They were at the house. I inquired at the house. They were in the *desk* in a lower drawer. I searched the drawer. Nothing there. I was about to give up in despair. I closed the drawer and happened to glance up at a pigeon-hole above, on the right-hand side. A paper without any envelope attracted my sight. I took it from its receptacle and hastily observed the word "heirs." I placed it in my pocket and at the first opportunity read it. There were just six words that gave me any intelligence to work upon. These were: "The Surrogate of A——, O—— Co." I inquired for such a locality, and after finding its situation wrote the surrogate there. He replied that he knew nothing of the matters mentioned in the paper I had discovered in the desk at N——. After some hard work and further search, I finally obtained the information that this paper simply referred to a division of money, part of an inheritance belonging to my father's widow, he having married twice.

I then went on a journey to examine the records in the county where deeds of property which had been my father's were on file. My mother's name—that mother whose likeness the quaint golden locket contained—was attached to a sale of property amounting to a small sum. There was a deed of sale of the remainder in bulk. I also wrote to the clerk of the county where my father had inherited this property from his father. There was no record there of any inheritance of mine.

CHAPTER XV.

A further "Test."

ON my return to Washington Mr. Altemus had left the city. I waited for his arrival in September and again went for a "test." This time a spirit manifested with an injured arm. That is (to the uninitiated) the medium stroked his arm, saying it felt as though it was dislocated and had lost its power. To me this was a good test of my father's presence in spirit. He had a paralytic stroke some time previous to his death, and fell from his chair while sitting in his office, injuring his right arm (the one indicated by the medium), and never recovered the full use of it. But the spirit was unable to demonstrate further because of certain "bad conditions" left by the previous mortal visitor, so the medium told me. I was requested to come the following Sunday.

The following Sunday I again visited Mr. Altemus. After some statements of a symbolic character, such as "I see a high wall which you have endeavored to tear down, but which is being continually rebuilt," he said he clairvoyantly saw a young man sitting in an office chair, one that my father was accustomed to use. "This young man," he said, "has a full round face." I asked him if he could see his feet. "Yes," he said, and described a peculiarity to which one of my brothers was subject, the result of an accident. "He is your brother (giving his name), and he has a great deal to do with your father's business." This was true. Then Mr. Altemus made a peculiar statement. "Your brother," said he, "has more to do with the locket matter than you think, and he will be the one to straighten it out for you. Your father (in spirit) is urging him to take some action that will place the property in your hands. Oh, I see the spirit of a lady robed all in white. It is your mother, for she resembles the picture in the locket, and she says she will assist you." I then asked the medium about the paper I had secured. "Tim" took immediate possession of him, and told me I had secured the wrong paper and that I was not quick enough; "but your brother," said he, "will surely be the means of restoring the property which belongs to you."

Three names were mentioned during this seance, "Cassard," "Cyrus Walker," and "Attorney Meade;" also a description of two houses, one a frame house painted light with green blinds and a gabled roof, standing on a slope of ground covered with growing corn; the other a dilapidated building without lath or plaster, and a chimney standing outside. This latter I recognized—my father having once exchanged for a piece of property in the West, and which he had renovated. The three names given I did not recognize. He also spoke of "Trenton." The medium I visited in June, mentioned in Chapter XII, said something about Trenton and of my father having had property there. This I knew nothing about.) With the exception of a few trivialities this was all. I asked Tim how I could repay him for his kindness. In reply he asked me to throw out a thought for the eternal progression of himself and the medium, that they might do more good for the world. I cannot mention all he said, and with this the seance closed.

CHAPTER XVI.

My Brother's Statement.

AFTER deliberation I wrote to my brother inquiring if he had any knowledge of any paper appertaining to property coming from my mother or any one connected with her. He replied that he had not. His letter was straight-forward, and contained no appearance of evasion. He had once searched, he said, among my father's old account-books and papers out of curiosity, but had never found anything relating to wills or transfer of property of any kind. After receiving his letter I wrote him again, asking him to make a thorough search. I also sent him a statement for his affidavit. His final letter stated that he had made a thorough search, as I requested, but nothing was discovered, and he sent me his sworn statement, as follows:

"I have never had any knowledge concerning any property belonging to O. W. Humphrey in any way, shape, or manner. I have never had in my possession any paper appertaining to any property in which he was in any way interested, nor have not now any such knowledge or paper."

Thus the original clairvoyant prophecy, "*Always keep this locket. It will one day be the only proof you have that certain property is yours by right*," remains to be fulfilled.

MW-5

CHAPTER XVII.

The Mystery of Life.

The still-born children of the sky
  gleam and glitter down;
And their riper brethren gaze
  wisely on earth's round expanse,
Where finite bodies are consigned to
  dust, or sea, or flame.
But do they know the secret of the
  countless dead?
Do phantom forms flit through
  the vaulted aisles of space?
The eternal stars but mock the
  impassioned gaze of man.

POE'S yearning to know the secret of immortality is the craving of all mankind. Men search for earthly treasures and are foiled by a missing thread, a trifle, after years of patient effort. But the value of earthly possessions is mere dross compared with the intrinsic merit of a message conveyed as evidence of immortality. Of far more value, then, is the *proof* than the actual thing possessed. In the common affairs of life we give ear to practical things. If the ghostly dead visit our mortal abodes, do they not preserve the practical attributes of their once earthly presences? Aside from supramundane phenomena, mortal senses cannot know that the flame of life passes on to another state of nature. The mystery of the marvels of psychism is but enhanced if practical proof be lacking. Apparently the vanished hand which Tennyson craved to touch has become a verity; the sound of a voice that is still has lent its music to the listening ear, it may be. The old query of Biblical origin—if a man die, shall he live again?—has been answered, it would seem. Nevertheless, as laws of practicality govern in the material world, so the mind cannot be satisfied without consistent practical evidence as regards the immaterial world.

The story of the tiny locket has been told. Was it the spirit of my mother who evoked the utterance from the lips of the clairvoyant? Was it my father's voice that spoke in my presence? If so, where is the thing spoken of? Where is that of which the locket is proof? For without that, where is the consistent evidence of spirit identity? If it exists, records apparently do not show that it does. In what manner, then, can the locket be proof? Does the story of the locket constitute an unsolved problem of Spiritualism? Time alone can tell.

www.ingramcontent.com/pod-product-compliance
Lightning Source LLC
Chambersburg PA
CBHW030008030726
47499CB00008B/2947